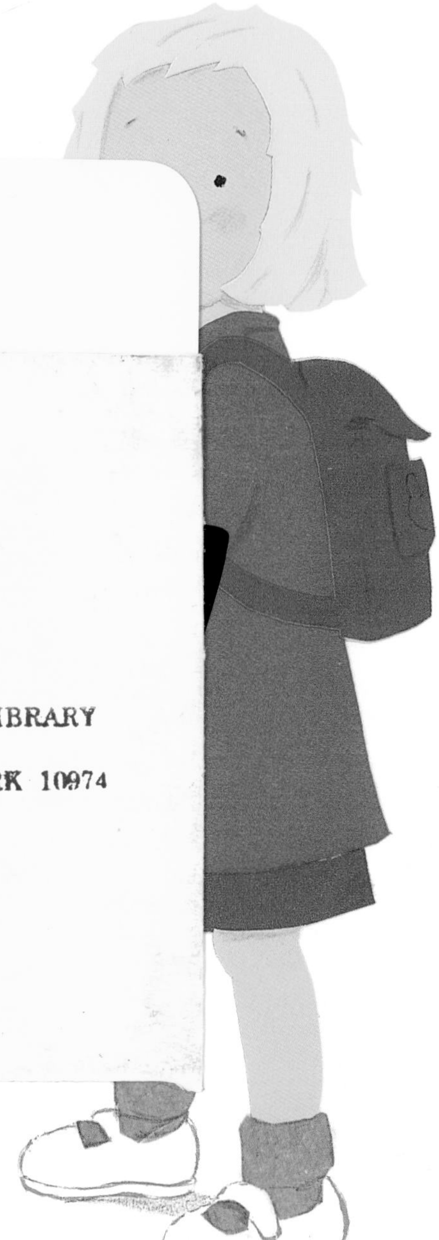

Illustrated by
Sheilagh Noble

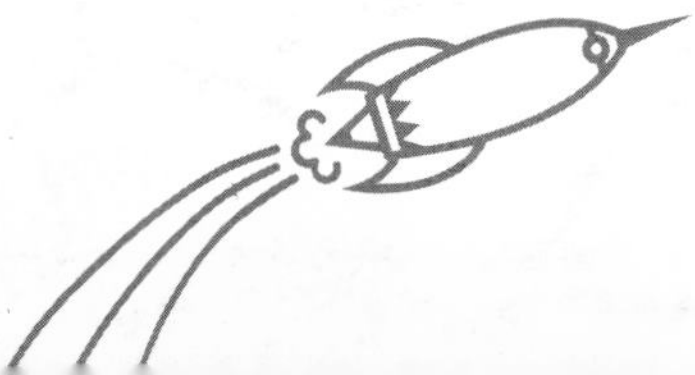

Here we are!

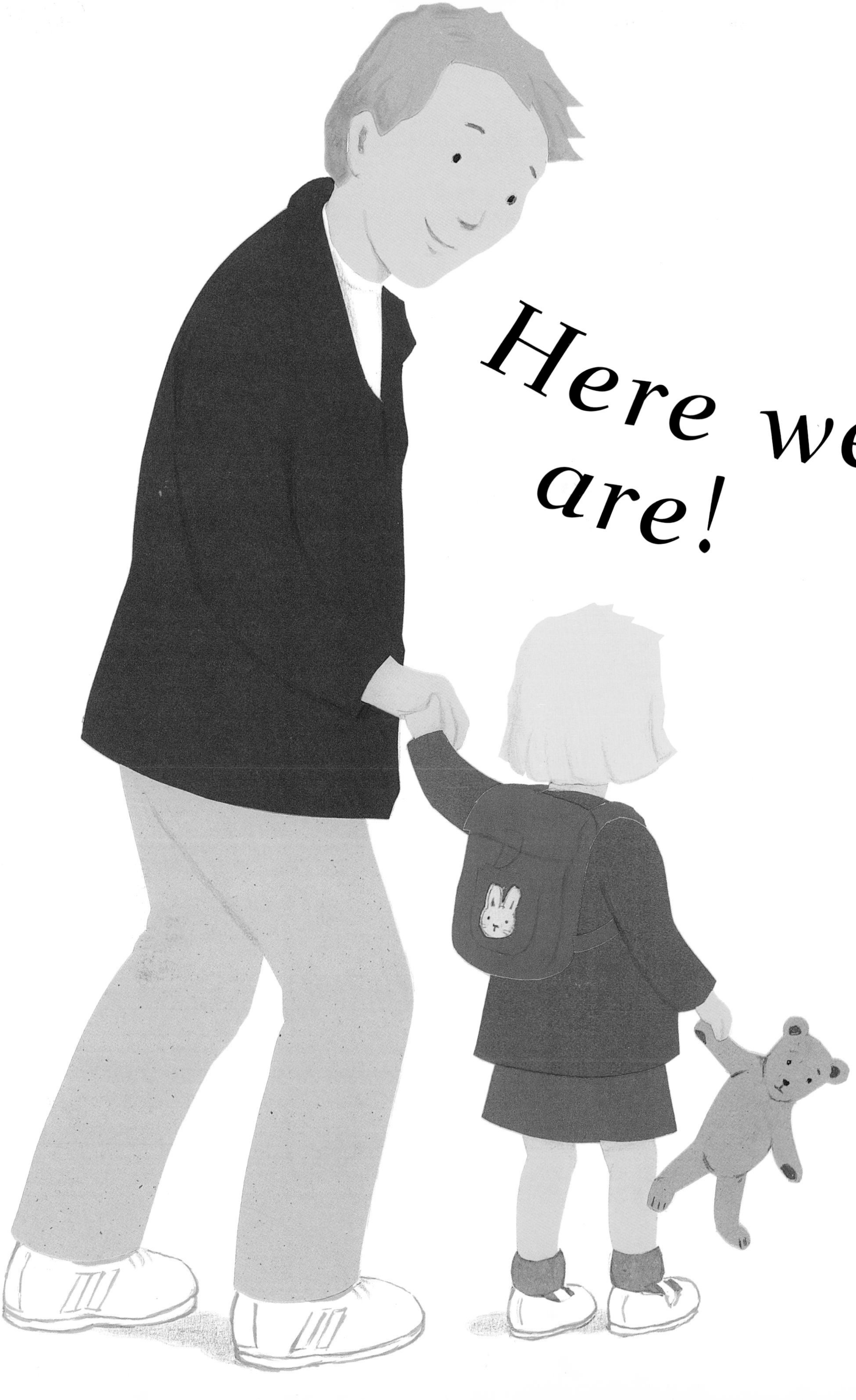

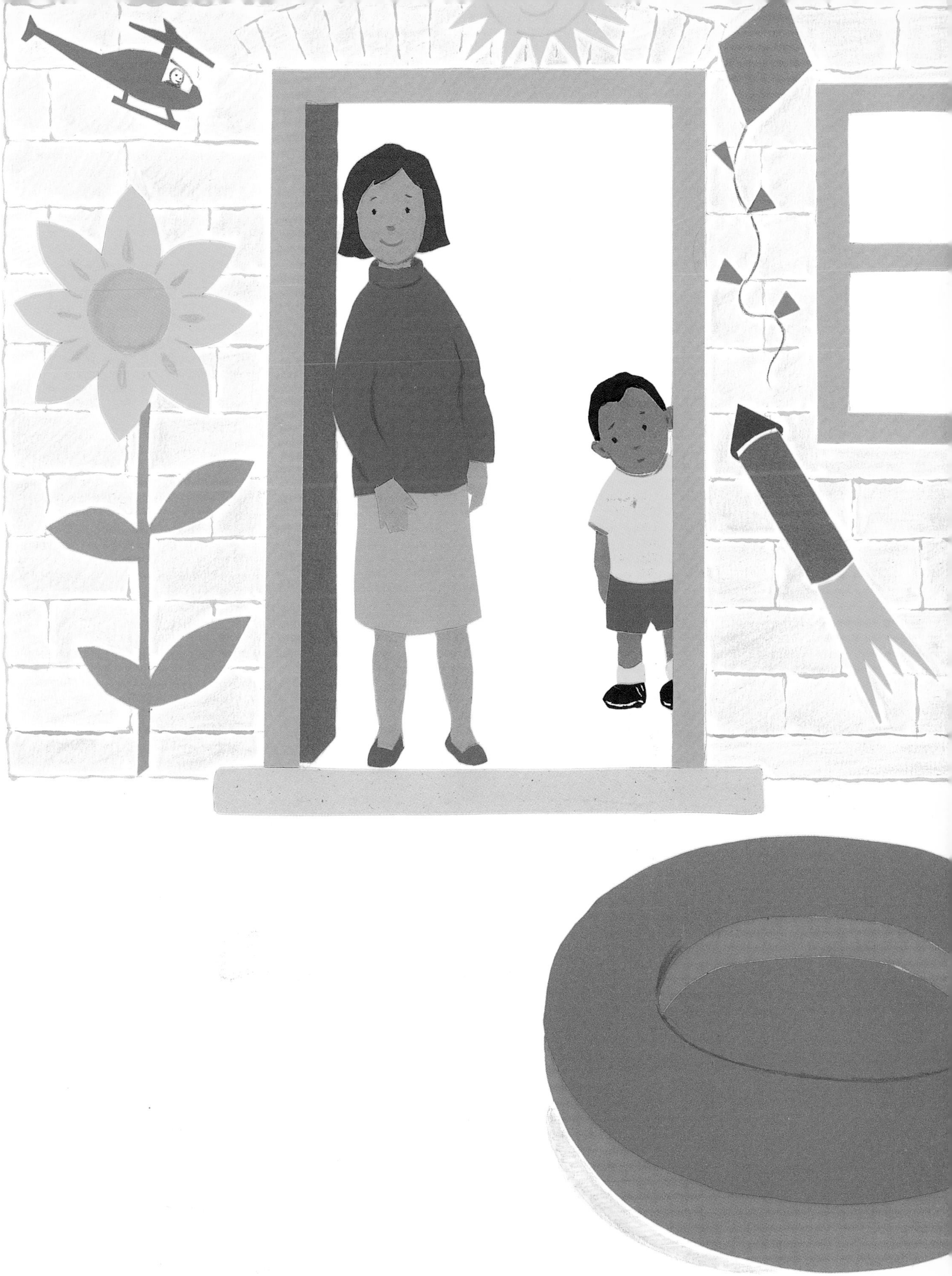

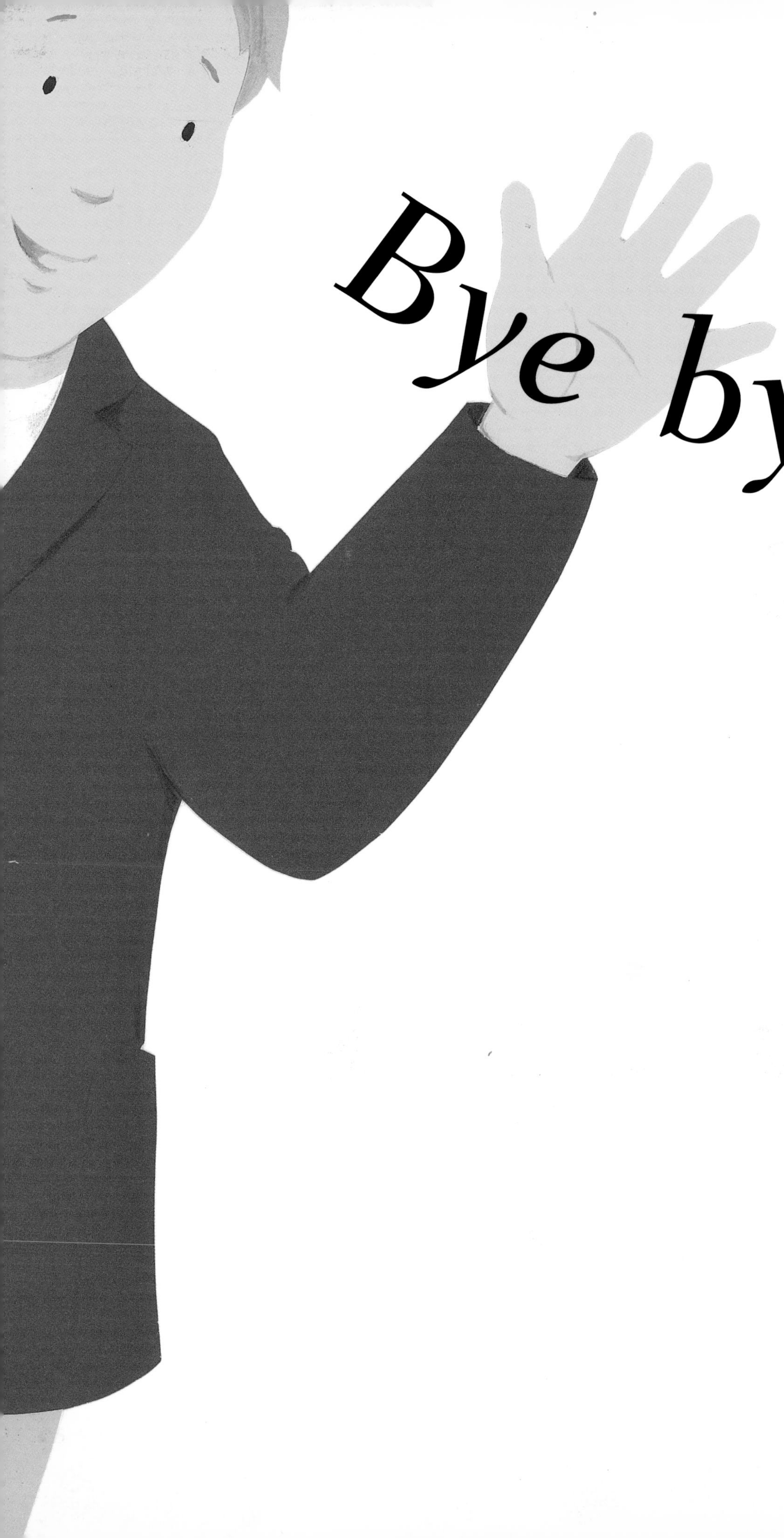

Bye bye!

Don't worry.

Bye.

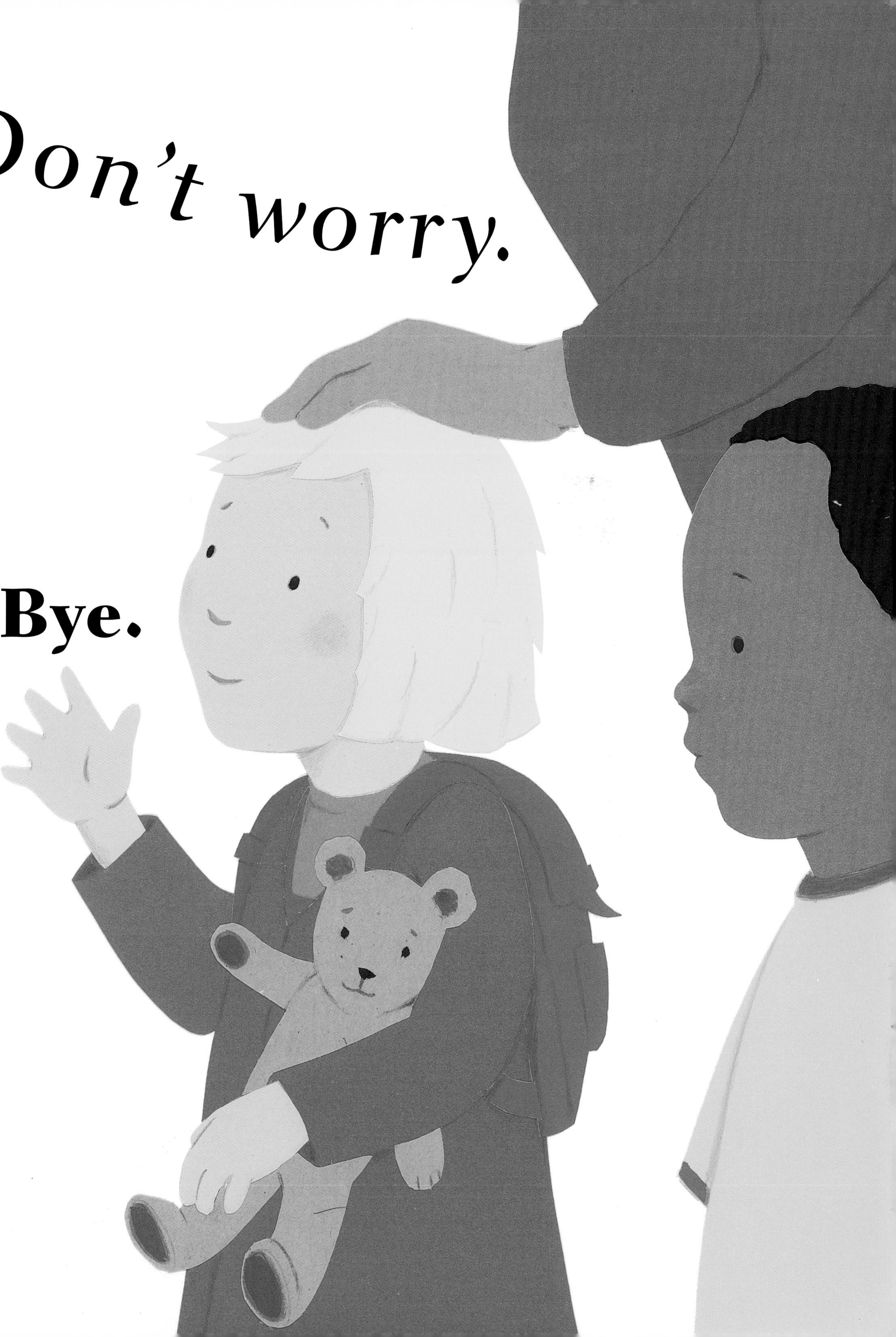

Look!

Mmm–red!

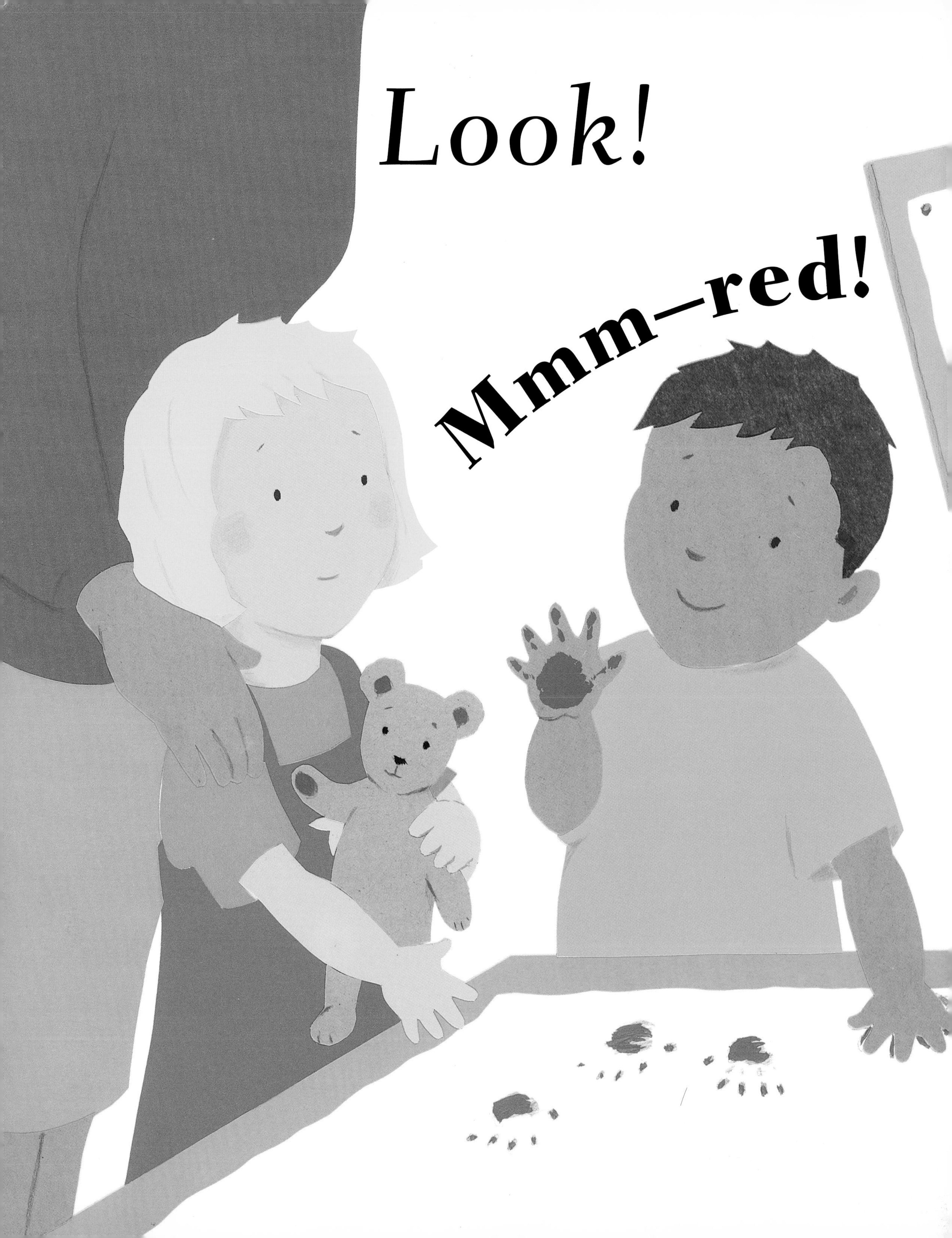

Uh Oh!

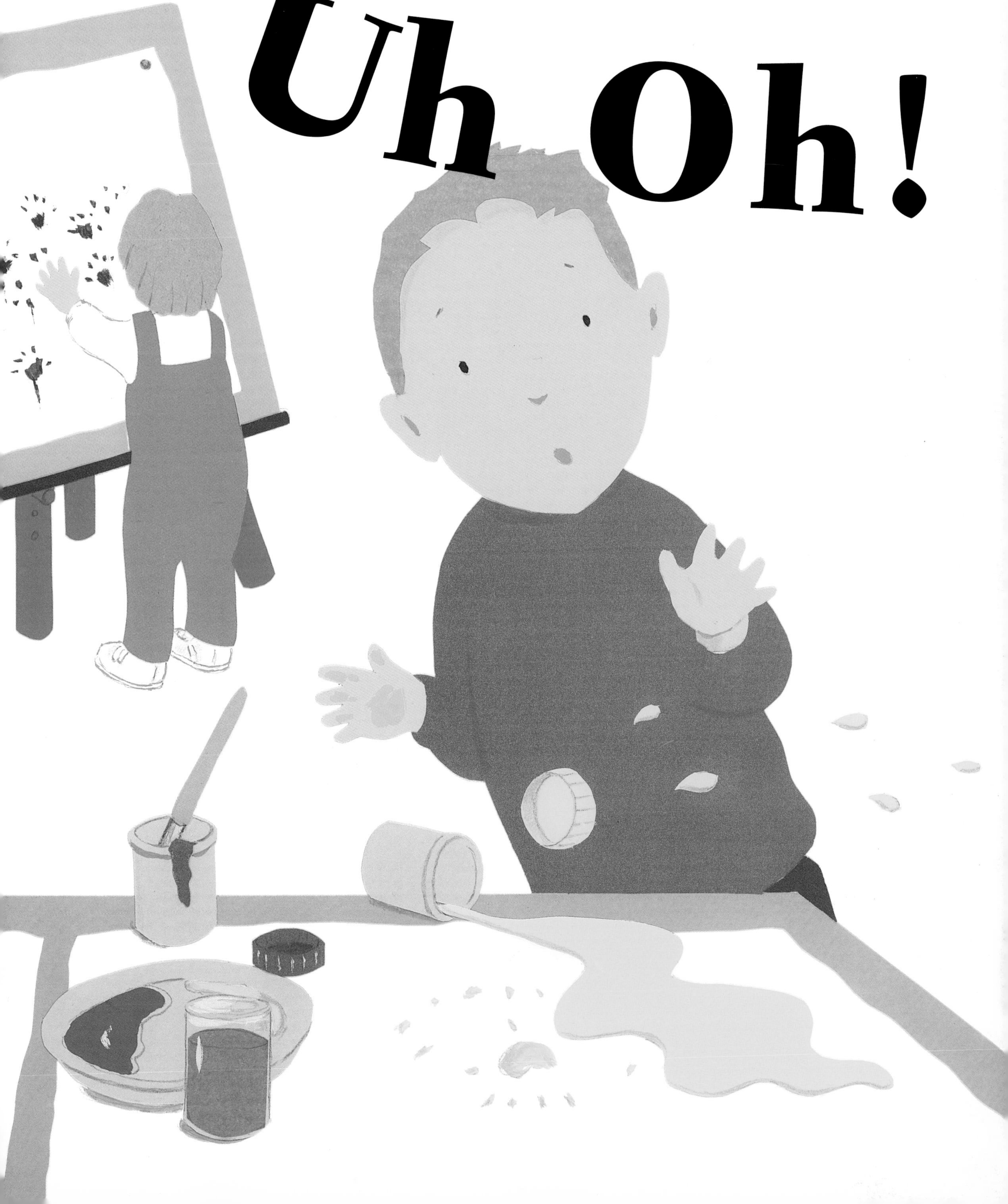

Mine!

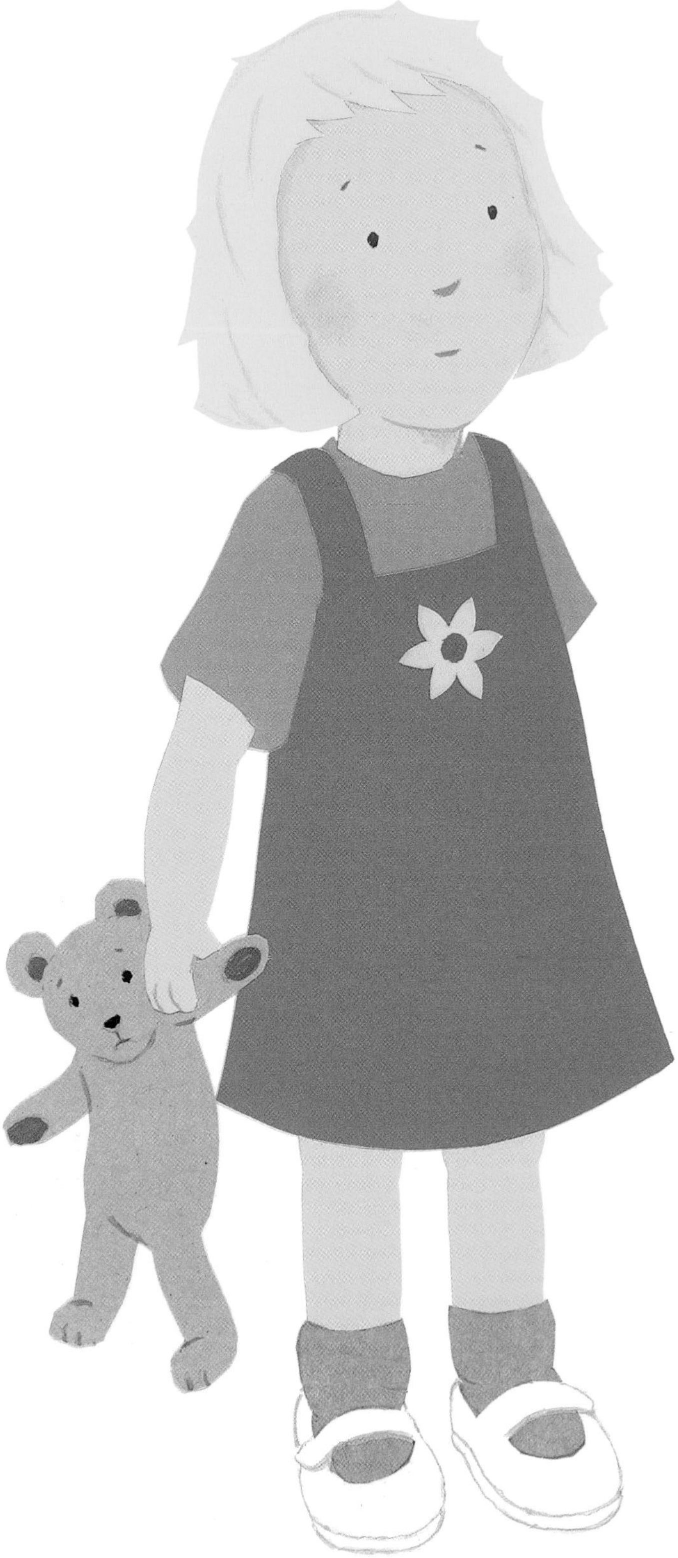

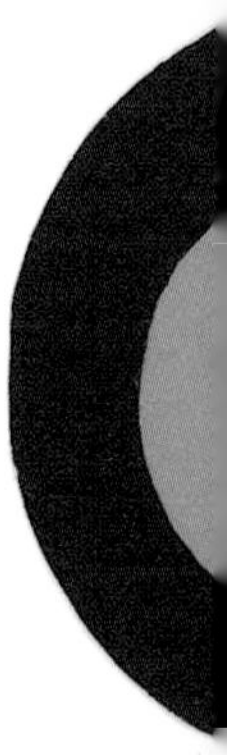

No – share!

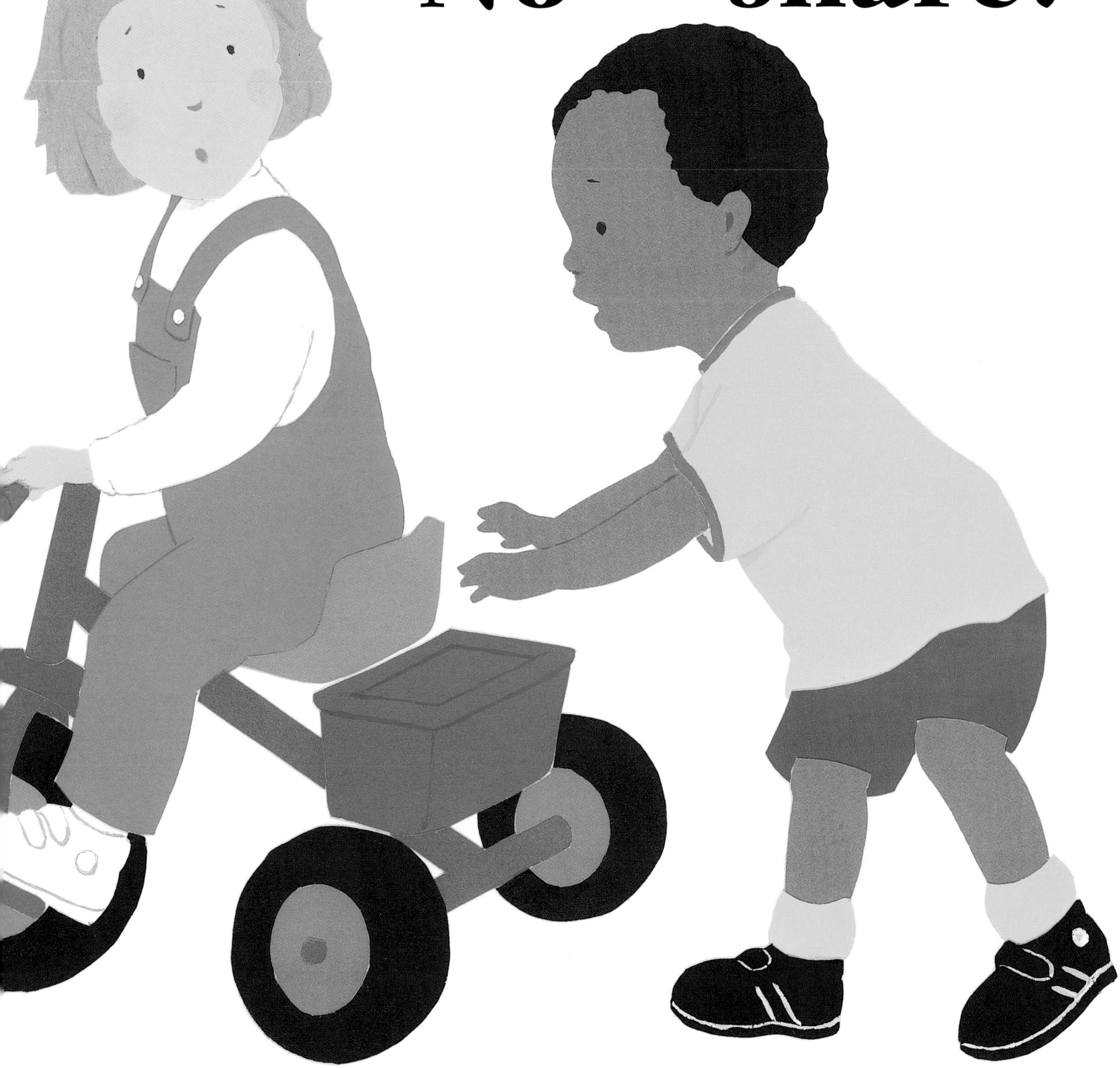

All gone!

More!

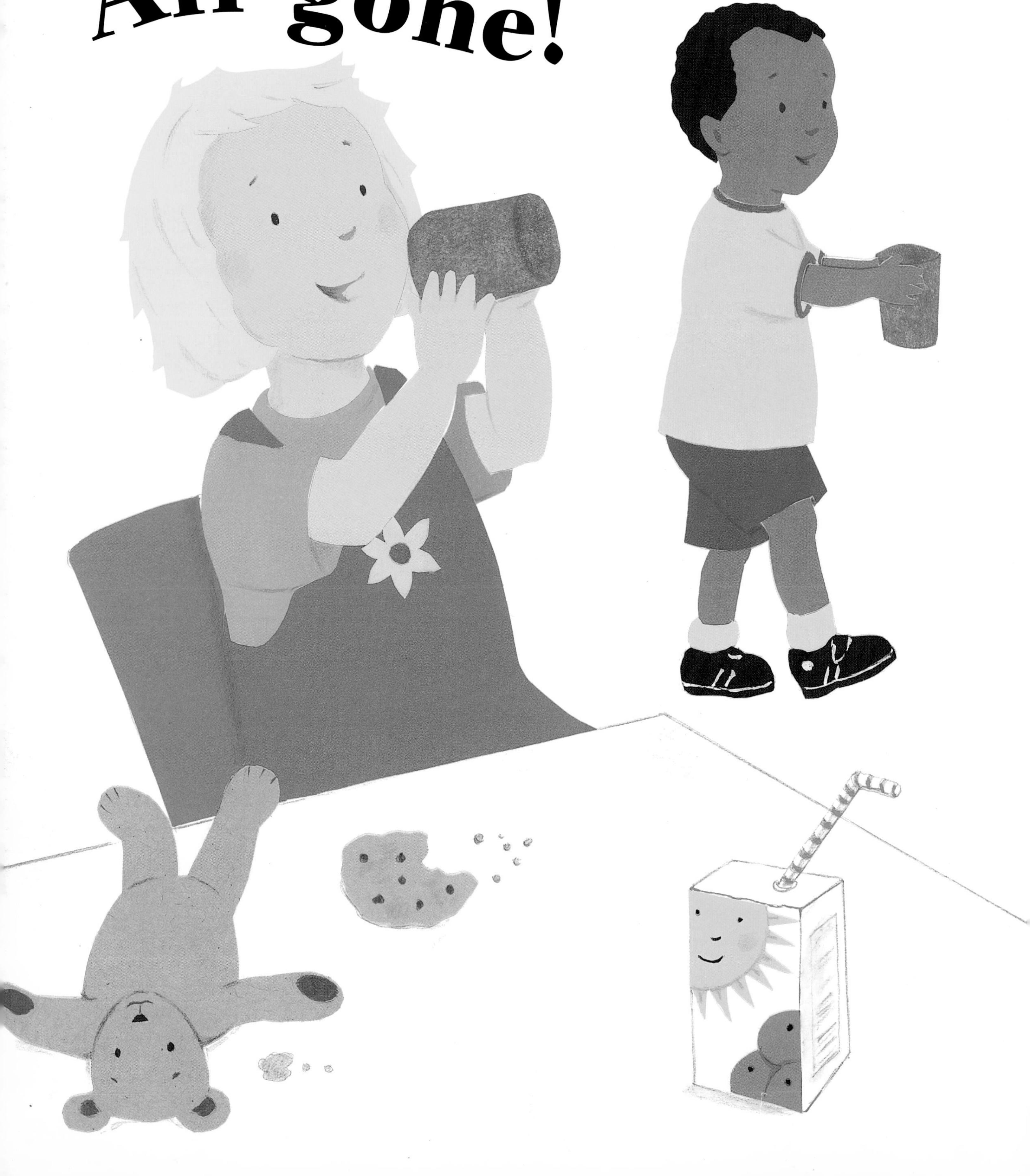

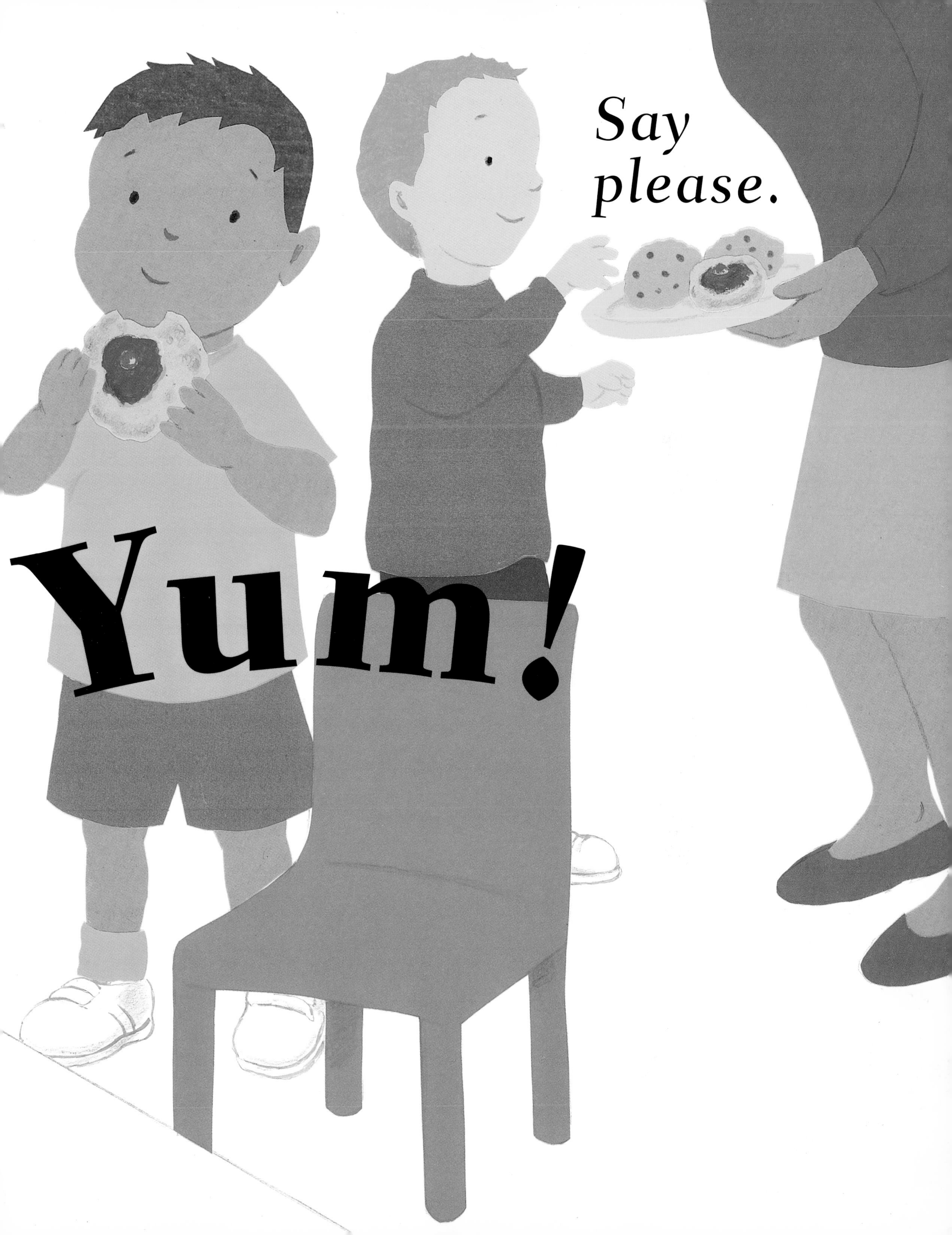

Say please.

Yum!

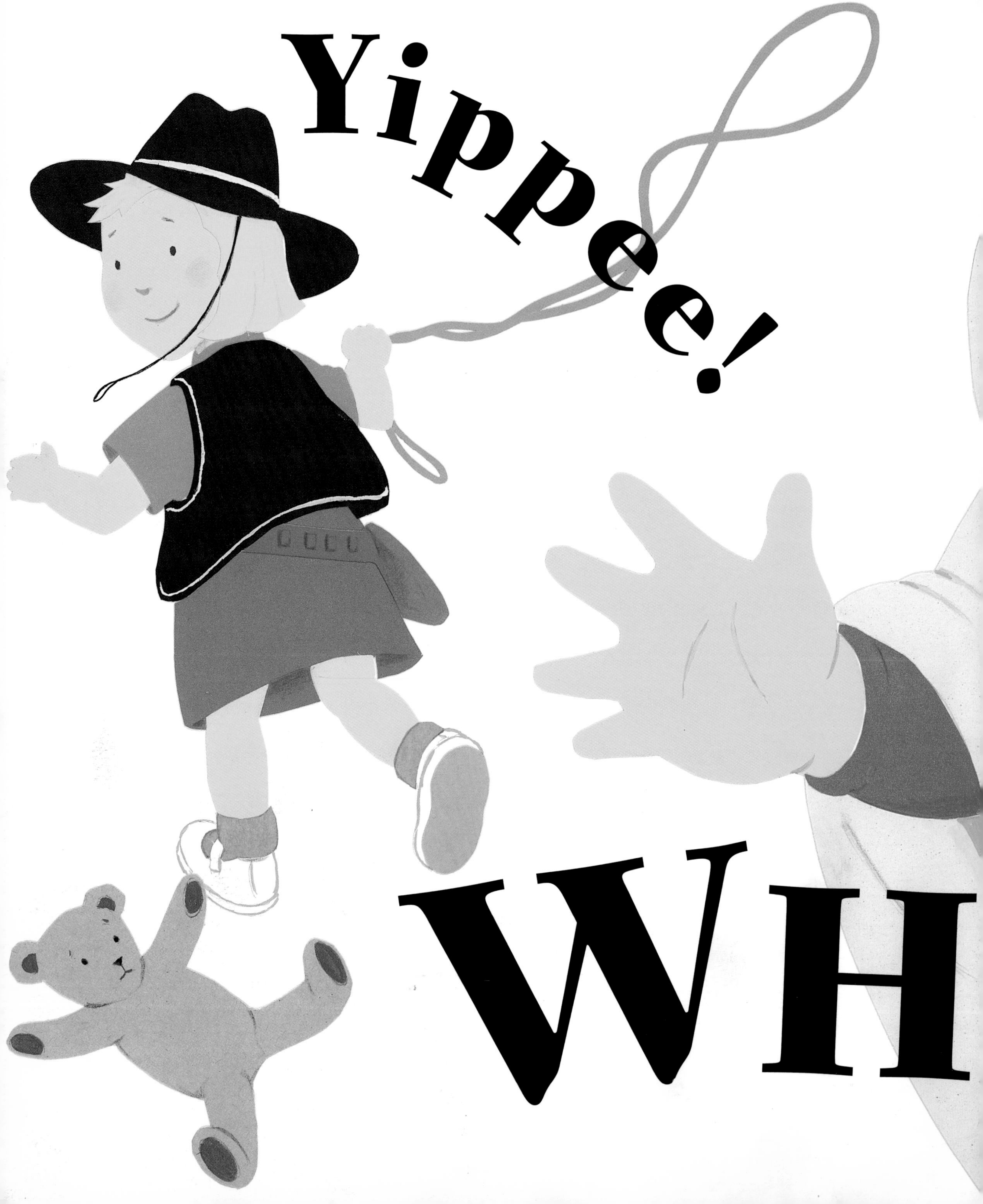

Yippee!

WH

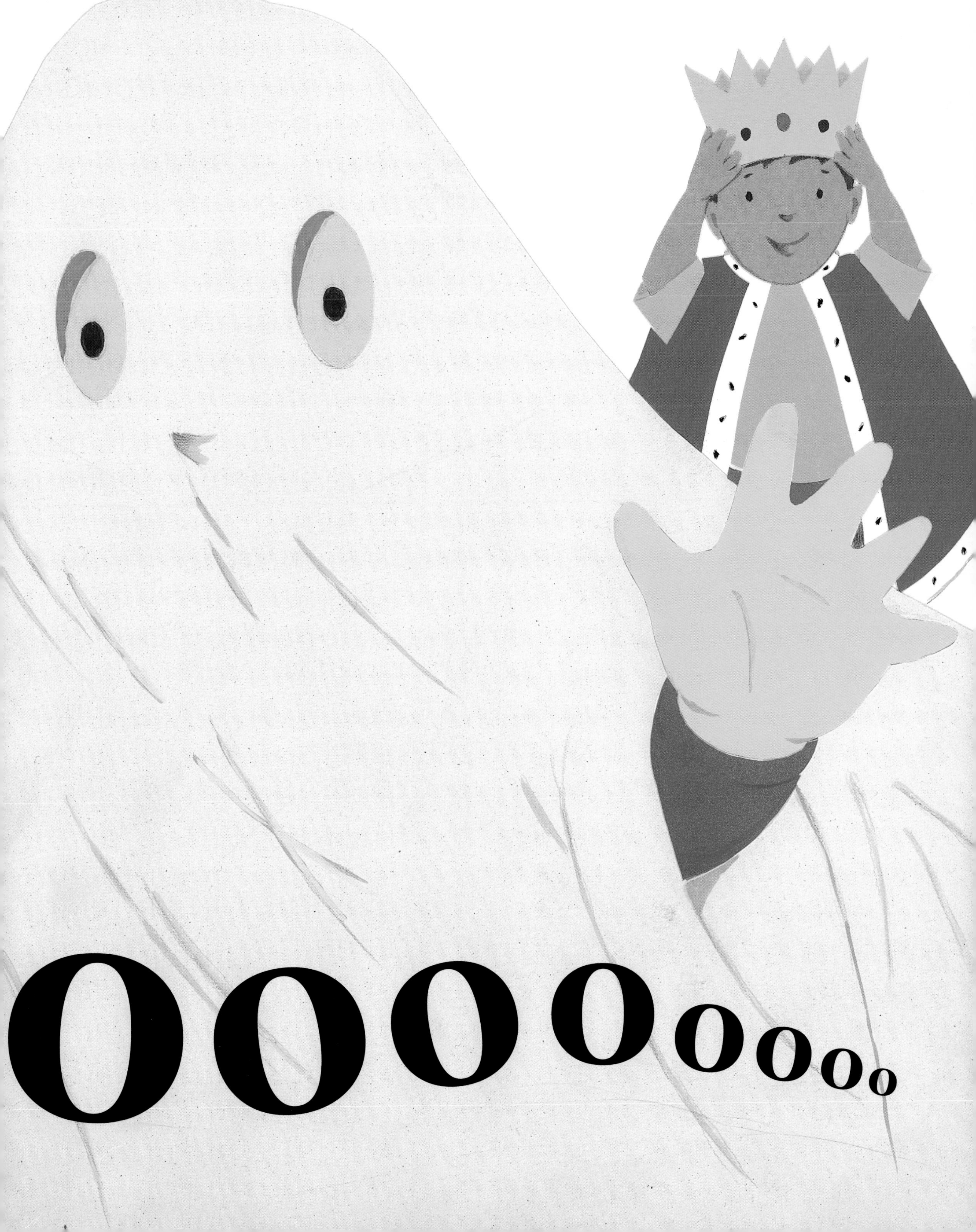

ooooooo

Once upon a time...

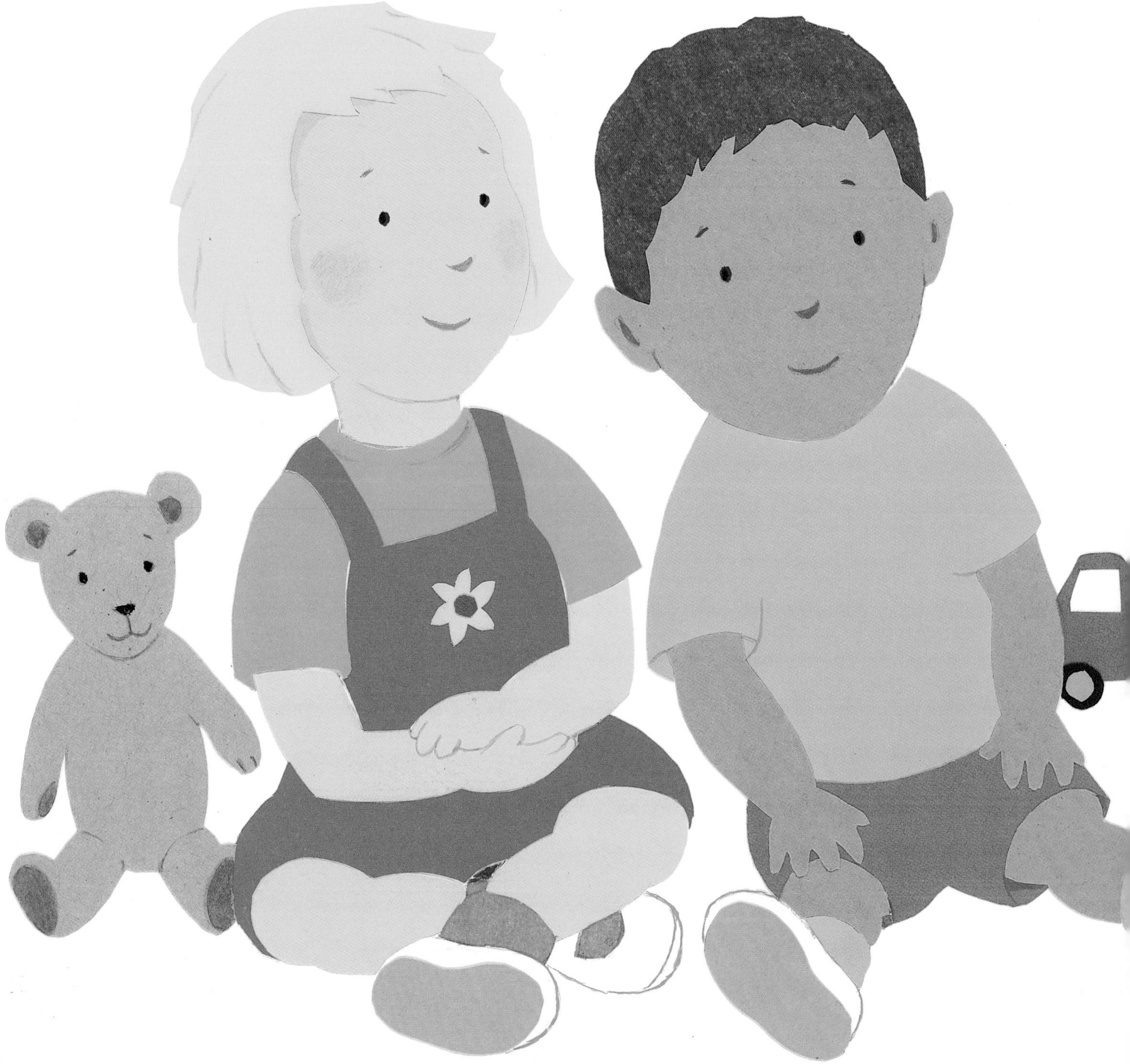

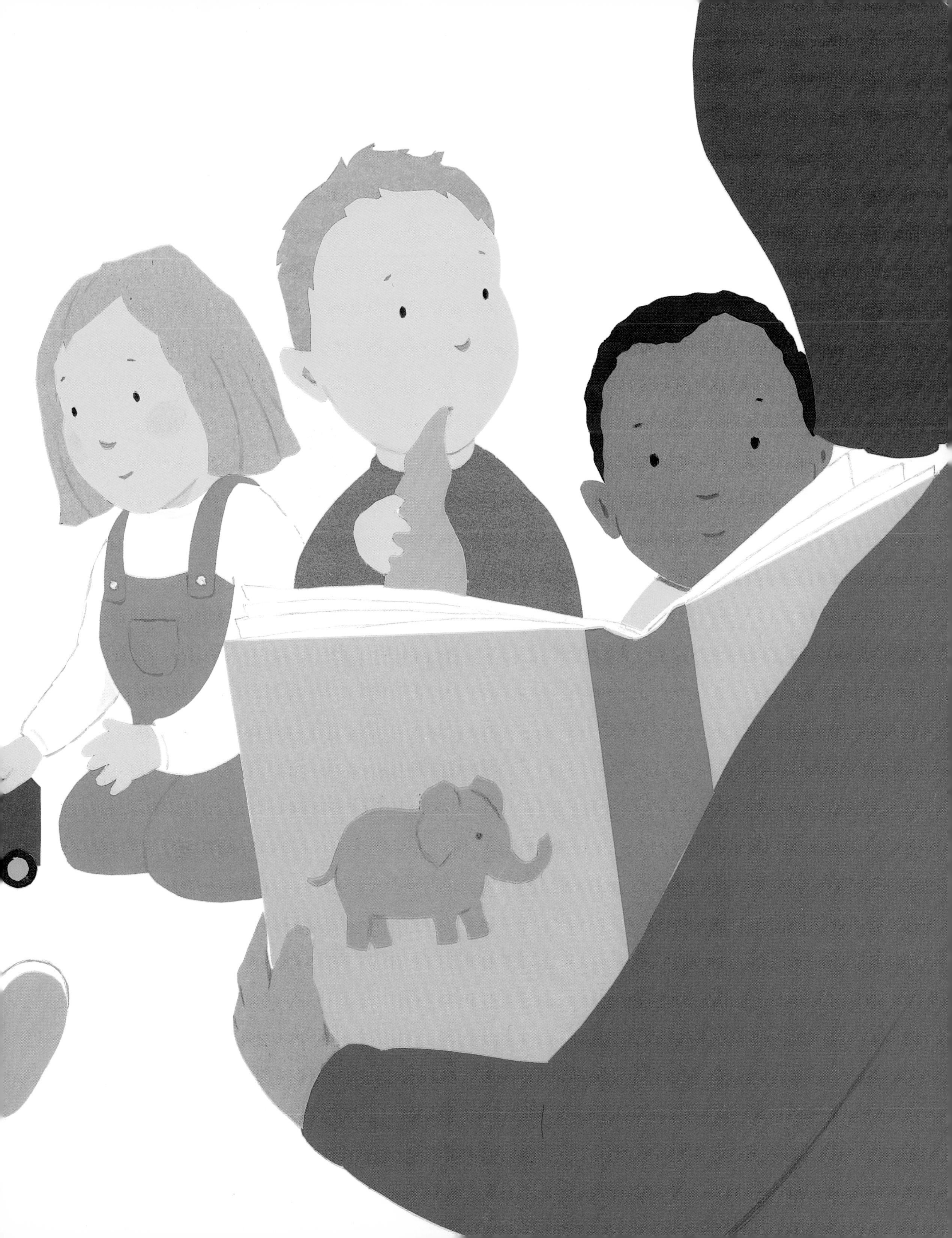

Messy!

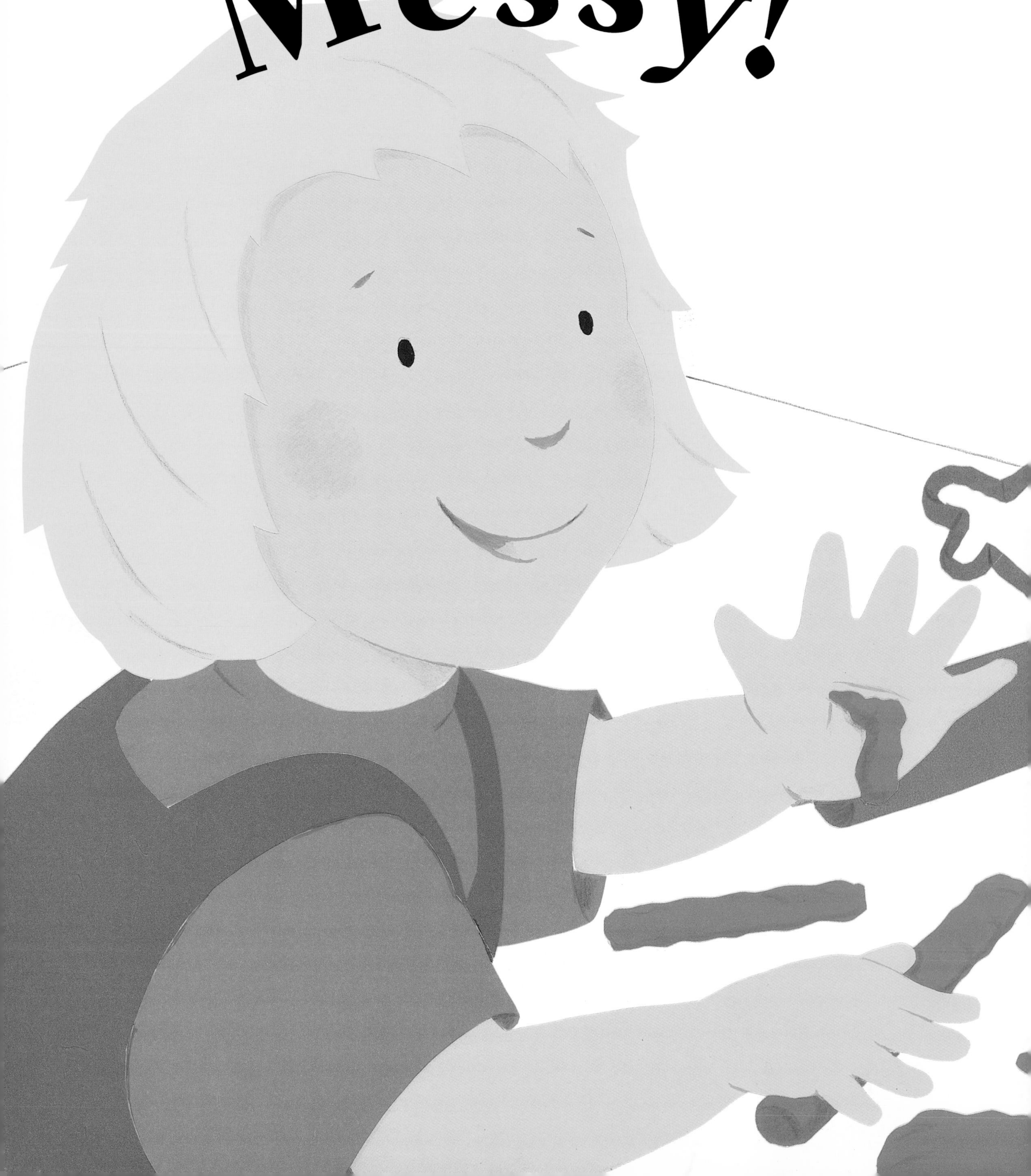

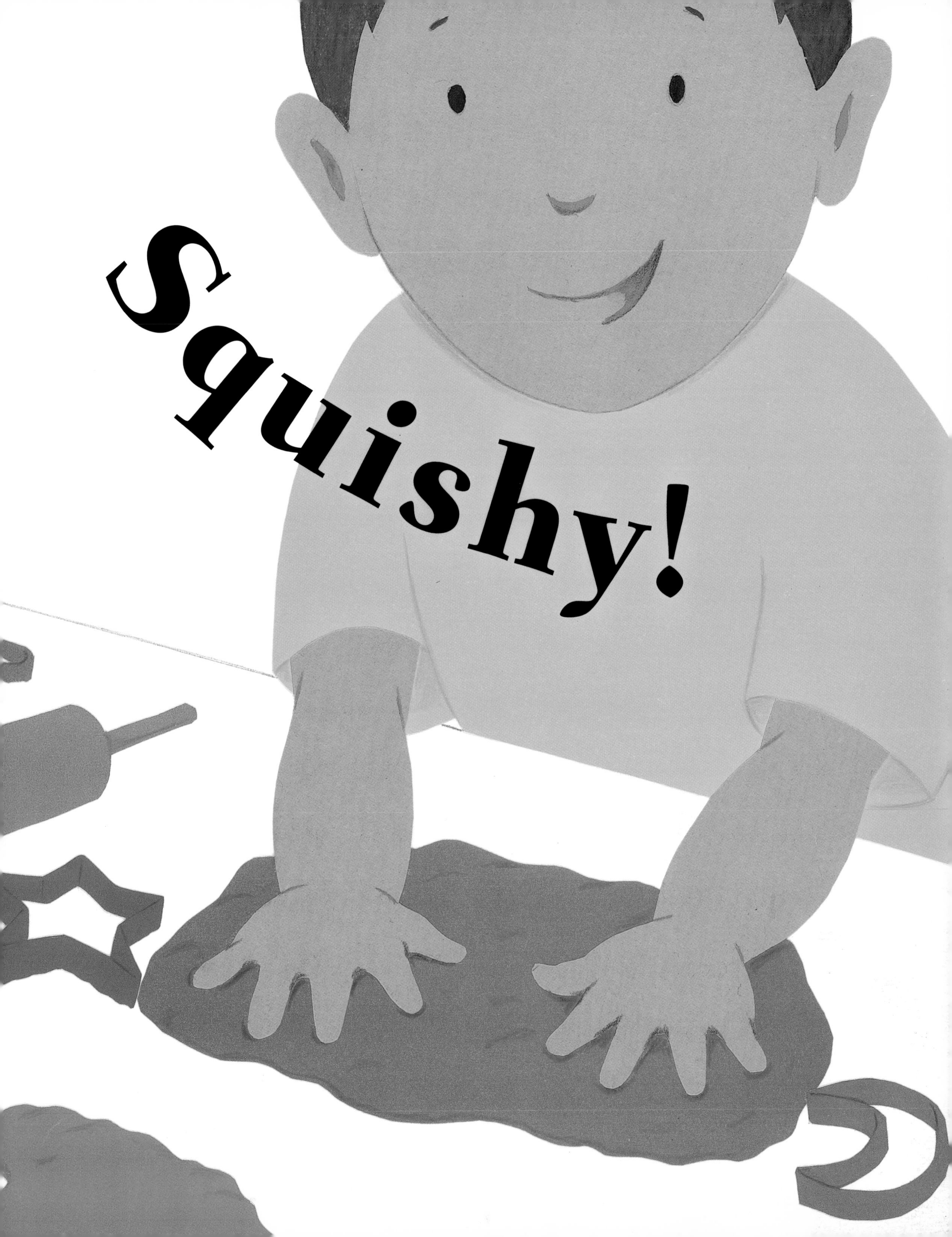

Squishy!

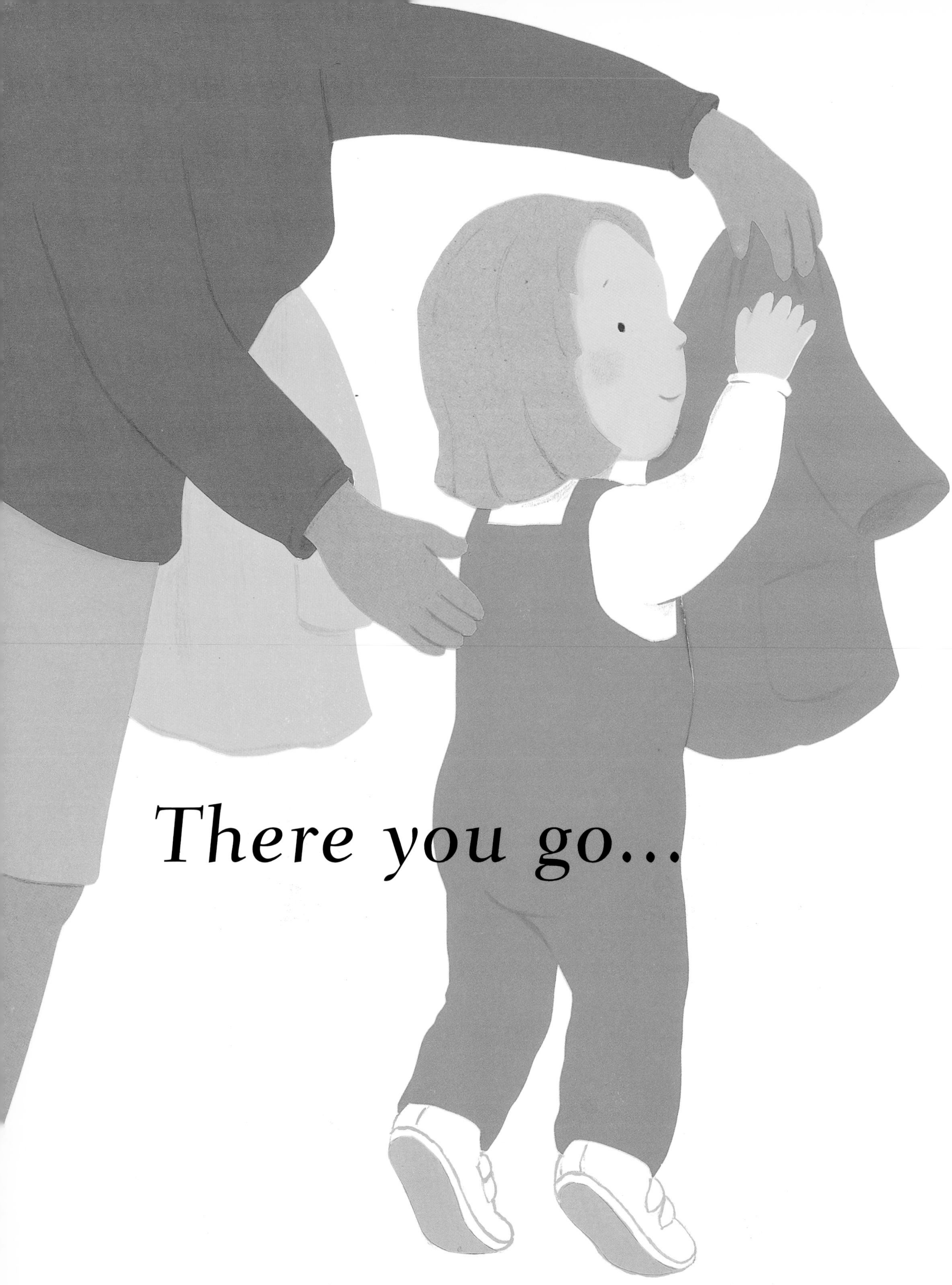

There you go…

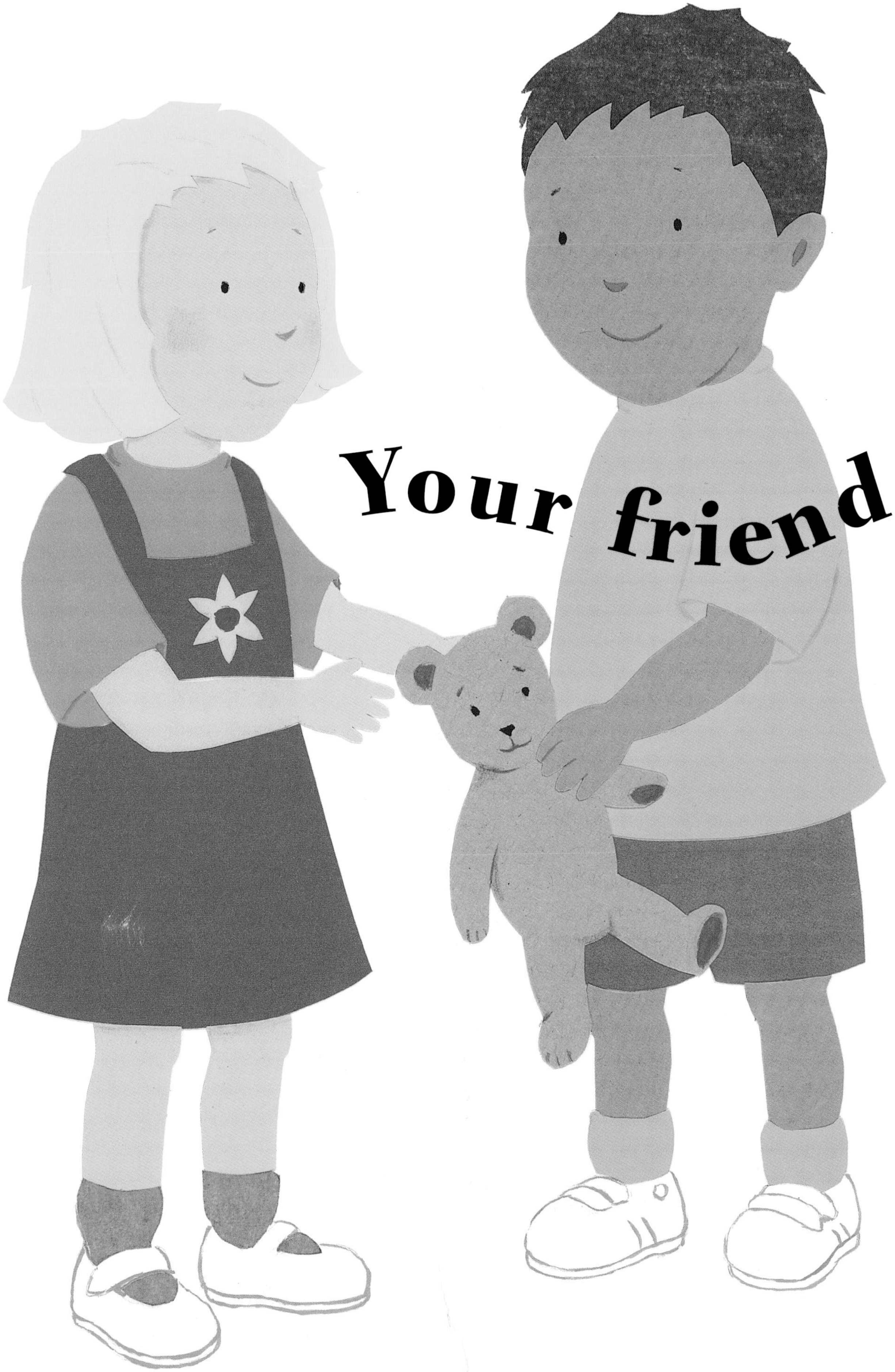

Your friend!

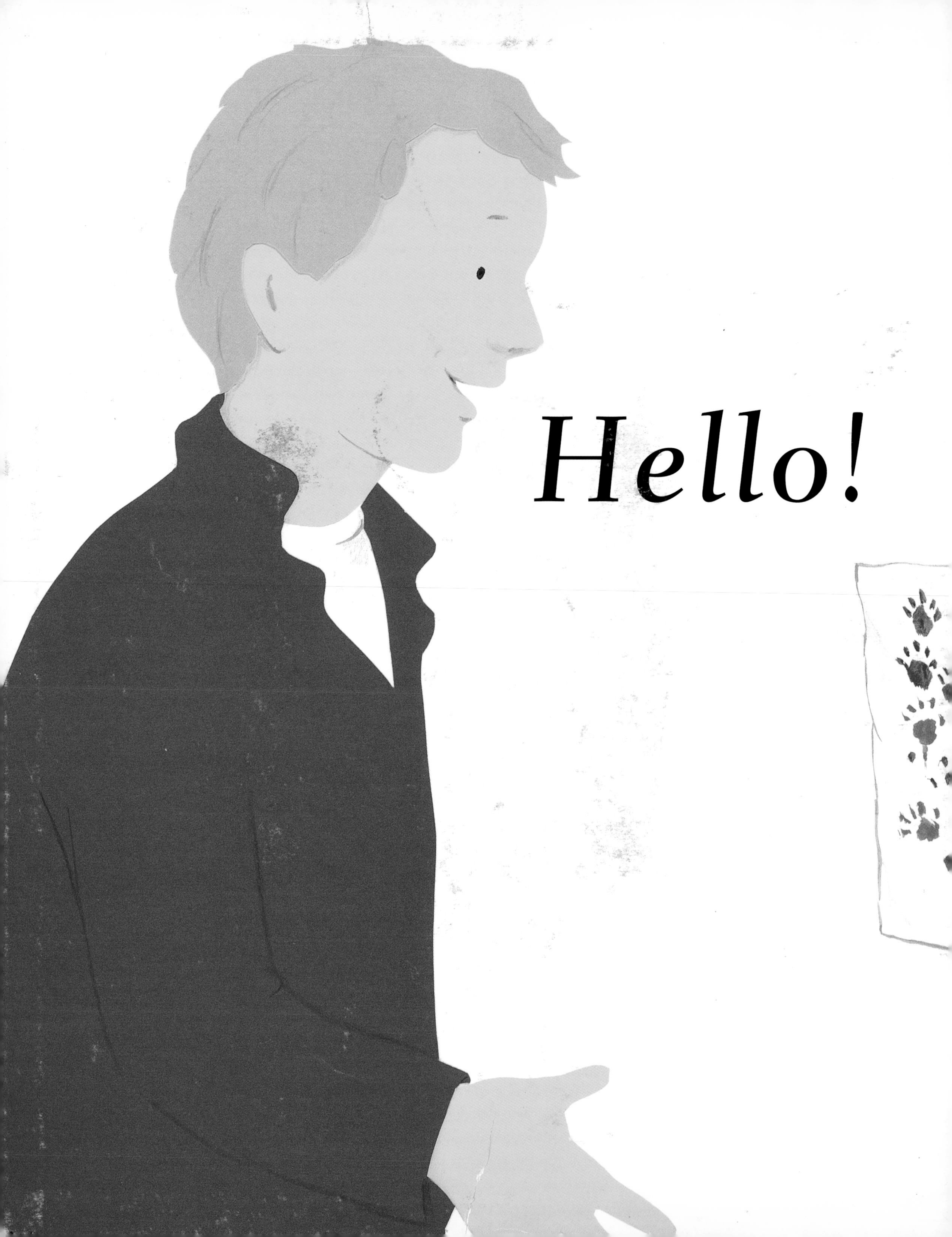

Hello!